FRIENDS OF ACPL

8/05

ABOUT THIS BOOK

No More Handprints is more than a story. It is also a keepsake you can treasure forever. Follow these easy steps to transform *No More Handprints* into a book that is truly as unique as your child.

In the back of this book you will find an ink strip. It contains an ink formulated especially for making handprints. It goes on evenly and washes with soap and water. (Disposable wet wipes work very well.)

First remove the ink strip from the book. Next separate the sheets of plastic to expose the ink. Set aside one half of the strip. Now smear the ink onto your child's hand. Place his or her hand anywhere in the book. Repeat the process as many times as you wish. Discard the used half of the ink strip. Now use the other half of the ink strip to make a special keepsake handprint within the frame on Page 1.

Be sure to keep *No More Handprints* in a special place. You will want to enjoy these little marks for many years to come.

Webster Henrietta Publishing

P.O. Box 50044
Myrtle Beach, SC 29579
(843) 236-0260
www.websterhenrietta.com

Book design by Sandra Wells

ISBN 0-9728222-0-8

Printed in USA

For information about this book and other products of Webster Henrietta Publishing, visit our website at www.websterhenrietta.com

No More Handprints

Michael Hetzer

Illustrated by Kim Clayton

Webster Henrietta
Publishing

Of all the mistakes the boy would make
In that house on Marlboro Sands
Nothing could get her quite so irate
As the smudge of her son's little hands.

On her white walls, oh, those filthy prints;
Fingers splayed like a spider or a squid.
He never knew what it was that made her wince
About those marks, he knew only that it did.

"No more handprints. No more!" was her woeful wail,
While off she'd head to the cupboard door
For the brush, and the water and the little yellow pail
To scrub and scrub till his smudge was no more.

Thoroughly erased, all sign of his being
Her mind again at peace, she'd whirl and scold:
"My son you must know that I'm quite sick of seeing
Your handprints upon my walls. You've been told!"

Well, he tried his best, he truly did,
But one day it happened on his way to the sink
After playing with a pen that had lost its lid
And spilled out on his hand a dose of blue ink.

He touched the wall by his bed, not hard, oh no!
But enough for that old handprint in blue.
His heart went cold as he imagined her woe
When she spotted this smudge that was new.

"No more handprints. No more!" she'd woefully wail
Then off for the cupboard she'd light
For the brush and the water and the little yellow pail
To scrub, scrub, scrub till her wall again glowed white.

He couldn't bear it. Oh what do I do? Oh what?
Ink, of all things... but wait, what's that humming?
The next thing he heard was the tell-tale shut
Of her door at the end of the hall. *She was coming!*

And that's when it happened, in his moment of fright.

He gave that old bed a shove, then another

Till it covered the smudge. You guessed it, that's right!

He hid that blue print from his very own mother.

She hummed into the room with a big load of clothes.

He tensed. Would she see the bed out of place?

She stacked his clothes neatly; he pretended to doze.

Then back out she went. Not a word! He was safe!

The boy was just six when he heaved that old bed.
And for the next twelve years he slept by the blot.
In all that time, not a word was ever said
Of the blue handprint. Soon, even he forgot.

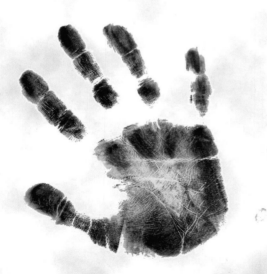

She sold the old house for a condo that was new.

And what happened next, perhaps it was fated.

They moved his old bed and there in fading blue

A boy's handprint imbued. He cringed and waited.

"No more handprints. No more!" Did she wail?

Did she run for the brush, the bucket, the pail?

Did she scrub and scrub to erase his spot?

No.
She did not.

She got out a knife, and with eyes that were red
Sawed a hole right through the white wall,
Cut out that handprint hidden by the bed
And took it to Florida. But that's not all.

The man grinned a boy's grin at what came to pass
To that old handprint that she took.
She put it in a frame behind anti-glare glass
And hung it in her condo's breakfast nook.

Imagine! His mother, who scrubbed with such fire
Who hated those dirty smudges most of all
Taking out a hammer, a nail and some wire
And *hanging* his dirty handprint on the wall!

So that's why I'm making for you this day

A handprint, a snapshot to forever recall

Me, at this moment, before time flies away.

(And so you don't have to cut a hole in your wall!)

Michael Hetzer is author of *The Forbidden Zone,* (Simon & Schuster) among other books, and is the founding editor of *The Moscow Times,* the first-ever English-language daily newspaper in Russia. He lives in Myrtle Beach, South Carolina with his wife, Tamara and children, Stephanie and Conrad.

Kim Clayton is an internationally-known folk artist. Kim's paint brush never touches canvas; she paints only on trash and dubs her method, *trash to treasure.* Kim lives in Myrtle Beach, South Carolina with her husband, David and their three children, Leslie, David and Noah. She prays that this book will help people to treasure their children as the true gifts from God they are.

All the paintings in this book are acrylic paint and airbrush paint on scrap plywood.